GW00865905

Unicorns love
AMELIA

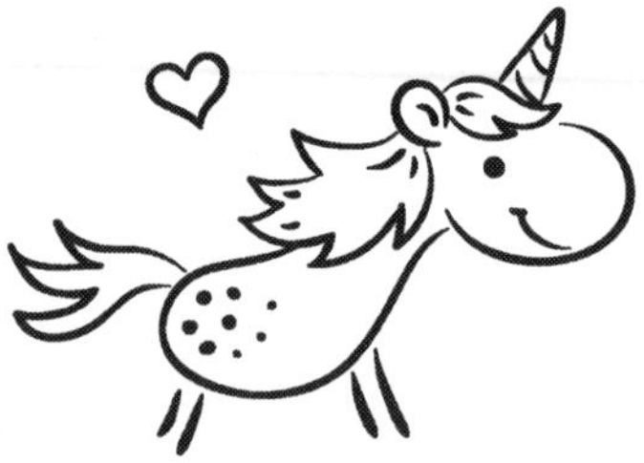

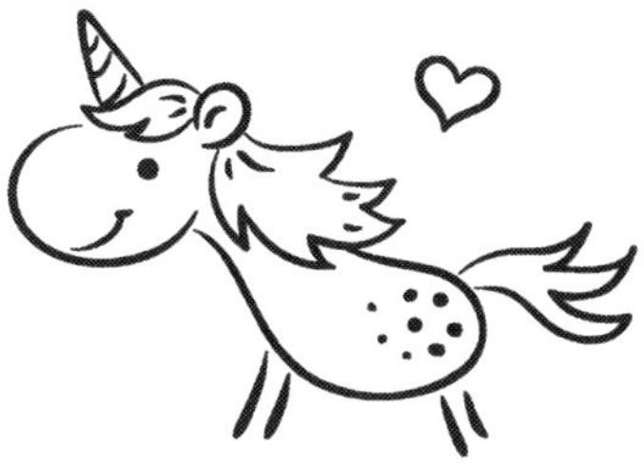

AMELIA & THE WISDOM OF UNICORNS

Coloring Book

C. A. Jameson

Amelia
is like a
unicorn; magical
and not afraid
to show it!

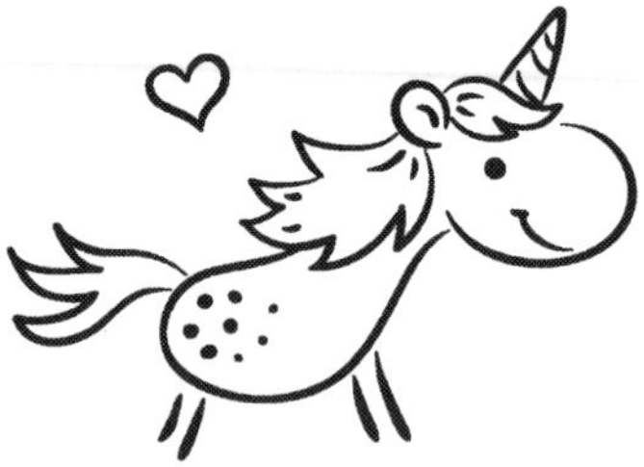

Happiness is
believing in unicorns.

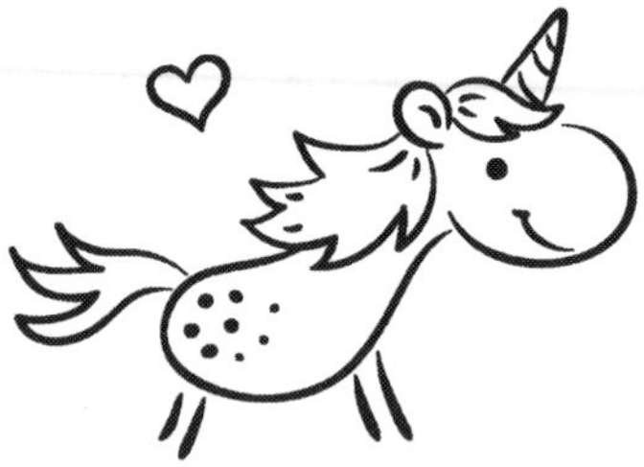

Amelia, have a rainbow day
filled with unicorns and glitter!

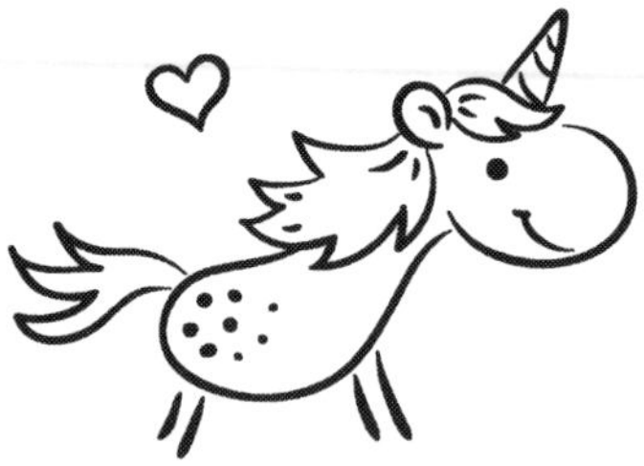

Amelia, your sparkle has not gone unnoticed!

Amelia is a
twinkling star!

Amelia is like
a unicorn; rare,
sweet, and beautiful!

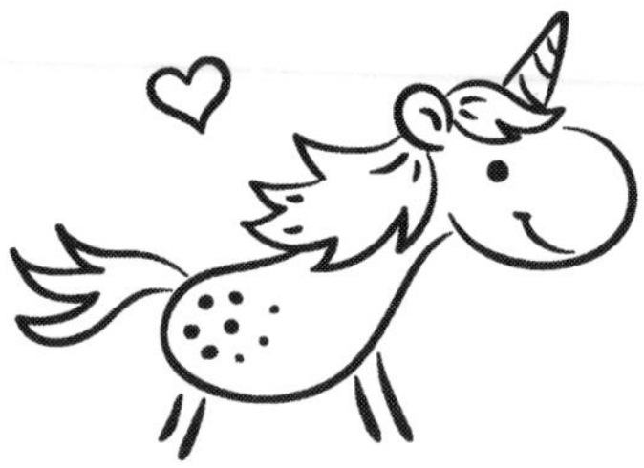

Believe!

Let your heart believe in
things your eyes have never seen.

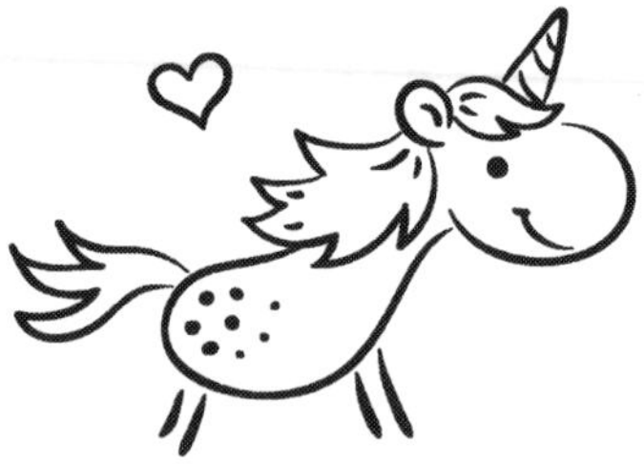

Amelia was born
to ride unicorns!

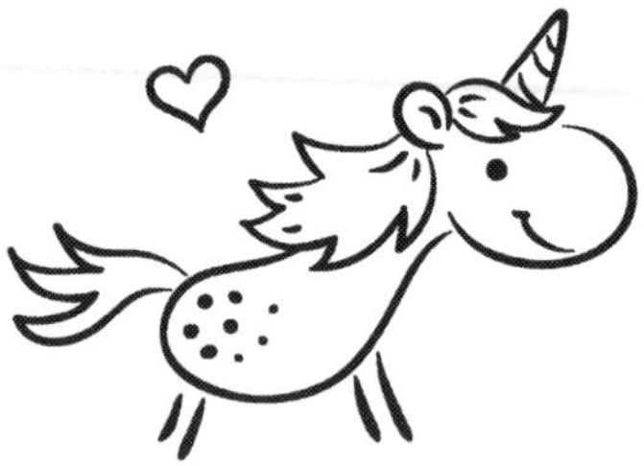

Don't let anyone
steal your dreams!

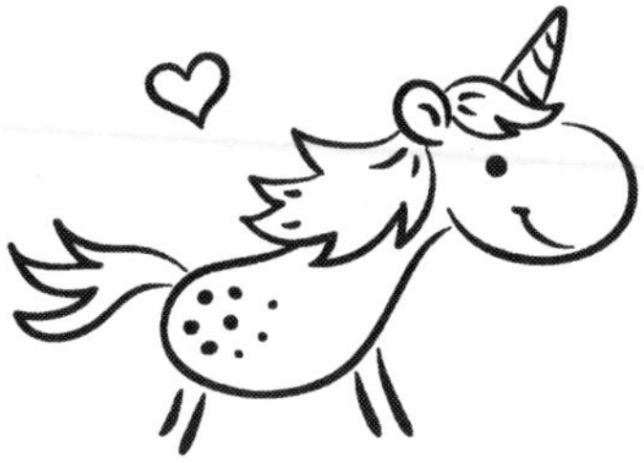

It's going to be a rainbows and unicorns kind of day.

Amelia
is amazing,
brave, strong,
and a miracle!

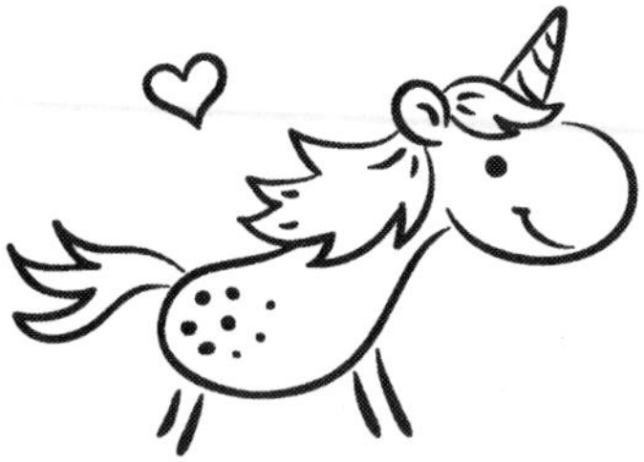

Be a unicorn in a field of horses!

Amelia is
as sweet as ice
cream and candy!

Amelia
sparkles from
the inside out!

Unicorns are
a blast!

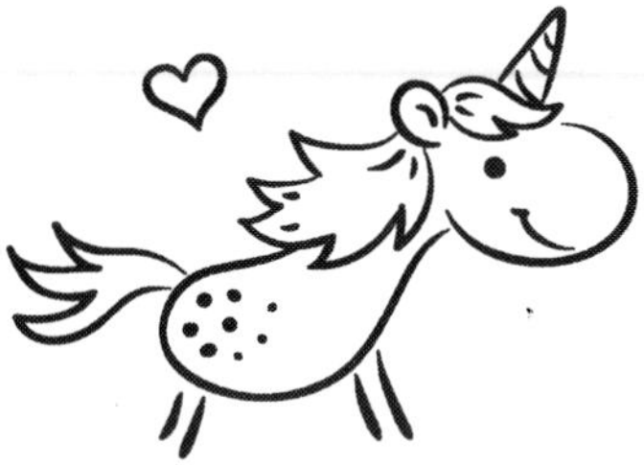

Play with fairies, ride a unicorn, swim with mermaids, and chase rainbows!

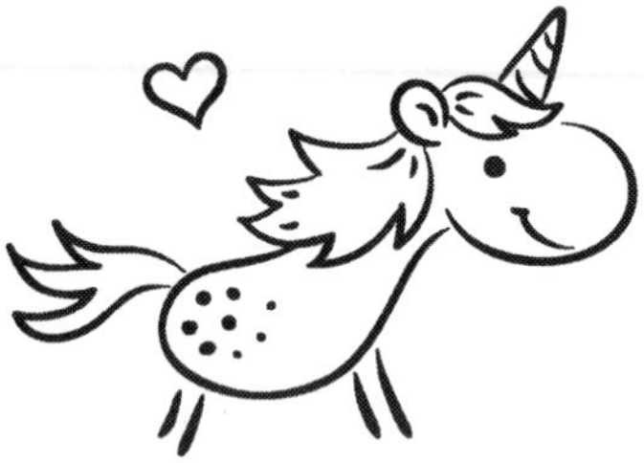

Today is all glitter, rainbows, and unicorns!

Personalized Books for Children
by C. A. Jameson

Over 100 names available...
Your child is the main character in each book!

Fun Storybooks &
Coloring Books About:

Valentine's Day
Halloween
Birthdays
Christmas
Easter
Rhymes
Science
Robots
Space
and More!

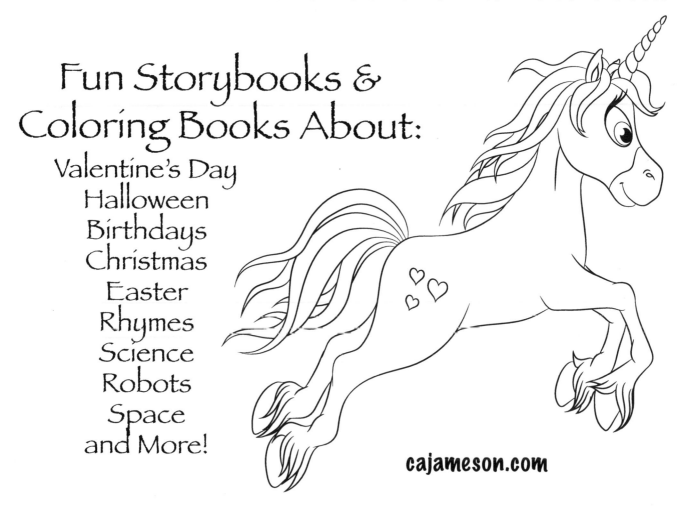

cajameson.com

Printed in Great Britain
by Amazon

33386346R00045